D1378561

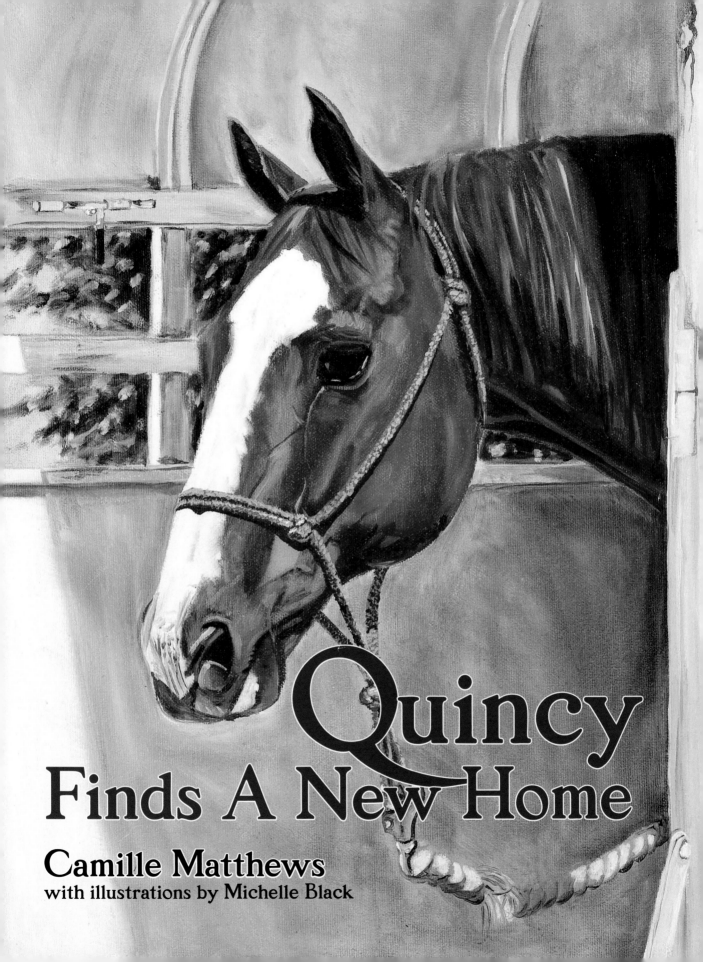

# Quincy
# Finds A New Home

**Camille Matthews**
with illustrations by Michelle Black

Illustrations by Michelle Black


Published by Pathfinder Equine Publications

1908 Glade Rd.

Farmington, NM 87401

Camille Matthews: pathfinder1908@gmail.com

ISBN: 978-0-9819240-0-7


Printed in the USA

The QUINCY THE HORSE books
are for my grandfather,
William L. Matthews, Sr.
my mentor,
Phyllis E. Schiff
and
my daughter, Lisa

—Camille Matthews

Quincy was a little red horse.

His coat was the color of a new penny.

His mane and tail were long and shiny.

His eyes were soft and brown.

On his nose was a long white blaze.

Quincy lived on a farm with a red barn.

In the summer the hills and pastures were green.

In the winter there was so much snow in the fields

that Quincy could not even go outside.

Nearby there was a forest with tall trees.

Quincy loved to ride the trails in the forest.

In the spring when the snow melted,

Quincy would go out in his pasture.

The owner of the farm and the children of the family

would ride Quincy to the trails in the forest.

Quincy was happy because spring had come.

The sun was warm. The snow was gone.

Quincy waited for someone to put on his saddle

and ride him down the trails in the forest, but no one came.

Day after day, no one came to see Quincy but

the neighbor man who filled his water tank.


Quincy felt bad.

Quincy felt lonely.

Quincy stood by himself at the fence.

One morning Quincy stood grazing in his pasture.

A man and a lady drove up in a tan truck.

They were pulling a white horse trailer.

They got out of the truck and stood at the fence

looking at Quincy. The man took out a saddle.

He put it on Quincy's back. The lady mounted up.

The man opened the gate and the lady rode

Quincy down the road into the forest.

Quincy flew along his favorite trail.

When Quincy came back to the road,

he trotted along the fences of the pasture.


Quincy felt happy.

Quincy felt proud.

Quincy pranced sideways.

Quincy stopped and
the lady got down.

Quincy saw that she was smiling.

The lady and the man walked
around Quincy.

Then they stopped and stood
in the pasture talking to him.

The man stroked Quincy's nose.

He talked to Quincy in a soft voice.

He said that Quincy was
strong and healthy.

The woman held the reins
of his bridle.

She said that Quincy was
beautiful and friendly.

The lady stood by the trailer. The man said,
"You are going to have a new owner!"

# WHAT?

# A NEW OWNER!

Quincy felt surprised.

Quincy felt confused.

Quincy spun in a circle.

Finally Quincy stood still.

The man took off the saddle.

He put a halter and lead rope on Quincy's head.

Then the lady led him into the trailer.

The lady said,
"You will like your new home."

WAIT!

# A NEW HOME?

Quincy felt sad.

Quincy felt mad.

Quincy kicked the wall

of the horse trailer.

The truck backed up.

Through the window Quincy

saw his red barn.

The trailer went through

the gate and drove away.

After awhile the truck and trailer

came down a long driveway.

They stopped beside a large barn.

The man and lady opened the door

of the horse trailer.

Quincy looked out.

There were people standing in the driveway.

They were smiling and talking about Quincy.

The lady led Quincy off of the trailer.

She led him into the barn.

There was a stall for Quincy

with hay and fresh water.

Quincy did not feel hungry.

Quincy did not feel friendly.

Quincy turned his face to the wall

and fell asleep.

When Quincy woke up he looked out.

Down the aisle of the barn was a row of stalls.

Quincy saw a horse in the stall next to his.

It was an old, brown horse with a white star on his face.

He was looking at Quincy through the bars of the stall.

The brown horse said his name was Beau.

His voice was gentle and kind.

He said that he would be Quincy's friend.

Quincy listened carefully to what Beau said.

He did not know what to say.

The new barn was a busy place.

There were many horses and ponies.

Every horse and pony had an owner.

Most days Quincy's owner came to ride him.

When she did not come,

a nice girl named Sarah rode him.

After he was finished,

he had a bath and ate some carrots.

At one end of the barn was a large building.

It was called an indoor arena.

At the other end was an outdoor riding ring.

The indoor arena and the outdoor ring were full of jumps.

They were painted white and red.

Some were small and low. Some were tall and wide.

They were for horses and riders to jump over.


The first day as he rode around the outdoor ring,

Quincy steered away from the jumps.

He waited for his owner to ask him to jump over a jump,

but his owner did not ride him toward the jumps.

She stayed along the rail of the riding ring.

On Sundays horses and ponies came from other barns.

The horses were tall and strong.

The ponies were small and fancy.

All the horses and ponies had braids in their manes.

A person called a judge stood in the middle of the arena.

The judge watched the horses and ponies jump jumps.

The horses and ponies that jumped best won ribbons.

The ribbons were blue, red, yellow and white.

The riders who won ribbons hung them

on the doors of their stalls.

The horse in the stall on the other side of Quincy

was named Triple Gift. Triple was brown like Beau.

He was one of the handsomest horses in the barn.

On Sundays, Triple wore a shiny saddle

with a white pad underneath.

He had blue wraps on his legs just for jumping.

The horse in the stall across from Quincy's stall

was named Mark. Mark was red like Quincy,

but he had long legs good for jumping.

He practiced jumping every day.  Every Sunday night

Mark's door was covered with shiny blue ribbons.

Every Sunday night when he ate his night time hay,

Quincy thought about the jumps and the ribbons.

Quincy was not tall and handsome.

Quincy did not have long legs.


Quincy felt worried.

Quincy felt different.

Quincy did not know how to jump jumps or win ribbons.

One Sunday night Quincy was so worried

that he told Beau his problem.

He told Beau that he was not tall and fancy.

He told Beau he did not have long legs for jumping.

He asked Beau how he could learn to

jump jumps and win ribbons.

He wanted his owner to be happy and proud.


Beau listened to Quincy. Beau was quiet for a long time.

Then Beau said, "Jumps and ribbons are for horseshows."

Beau told Quincy he had gone to many horseshows.

Beau told Quincy that he used to have a shiny saddle

with a white pad and blue wraps just for jumping.

Beau said that he had jumped many jumps and won many ribbons.

Beau said that he had won as many blue ribbons as Mark.


Quincy stared.

Quincy was amazed.

Quincy could not believe it.

Then Beau told Quincy that Quincy's owner was Beau's owner too.
Beau said, "You do not need to jump jumps or win ribbons. She just
wants a good horse to ride and love and be her friend."

Quincy felt happy.

Quincy felt safe.

Quincy lay down on the floor of his stall and went to sleep.